The Scarecrows' Wedding

By Julia Donaldson

Illustrated by Axel Scheffler

Scholastic Canada Ltd.

Toronto New York London Auckland Sydney
Mexico City New Delhi Hong Kong Buenos Aires

Betty O'Barley and Harry O'Hay

Were scarecrows. (They scared lots of crows every day.)

Harry loved Betty, and Betty loved Harry,
So Harry said, "Betty, my beauty, let's marry!
Let's have a wedding, the best wedding yet,
A wedding that no one will ever forget."

Betty agreed, so they hugged and they kissed.
Then Betty said, "Harry, dear, let's make a list."

"Just as you say,"
    answered Harry O'Hay,
So they wrote down the
    Things they would
        Need on the Day:

A dress of
white feathers

a necklace
of shells

Lots of
pink flowers

two rings

and some
bells

Then Harry gave
    Betty O'Barley his arm
And the scarecrows set off
    on a hunt round the farm.

They hadn't gone far when they spotted some geese.

"Oh, geese, if you'll give us a feather apiece,

You can come to our wedding, the best wedding yet,

The wedding that no one will ever forget."

"We will," honked the geese, and they each gave a feather.

(A spider friend
offered to sew
them together.)

"Hooray!" cried the scarecrows.
   They hugged and they kissed,
And they hurried back home
   and crossed "dress" off their list.

Then Harry gave
   Betty O'Barley his arm,
And they set off once more
   on their hunt round the farm.

They hadn't gone far when some cows gathered round,
And the bells round their necks made a wonderful sound.
Ring-a-ding ding! Ring-a-ding ding!

"Oh, cows, will you please come and make your bells ring
For our wonderful wedding, the best wedding yet,
The wedding that no one will ever forget?"

"Yes," mooed the cows. "We can tinkle our bells."

Then a crab scuttled up
with a necklace of shells!

Some mice found two rings
in a bin. (They were certain
The rings had belonged
to an old farmhouse curtain.)

"Hooray!" cried the scarecrows.

They hugged and they kissed.

"Pink flowers are the only things left on our list."

Then Harry said, "Betty, dear, I can find those.

Why don't I pick some while you have a doze?"

"Pink flowerzzz? Pink flowerzzz?"

buzzed a big stripy bee.

"I can find you a field of pink flowerzzz!

Follow me."

So the bee led the way, and they travelled for hours
Till they came to a field full of pretty pink flowers.

Harry stood thinking. "I won't pick them yet.
I'll need to find water, to keep their stalks wet."

"Just follow me,"
    croaked a lumpy old toad.
"There's a lovely wet pool
    at the top of this road."

They climbed up the road.

It was terribly steep.

"I'm tired," said the toad, so they stopped for a sleep.

Early next morning they came to the pool.
"This water," said Harry, "is beautifully cool,
But now I need something to carry it in —
A jug or a vase or a cup or a tin."

"I think I can help," said a slithery snail.
"I can show you the way to a very fine pail."

So the snail and the scarecrow
set off on their way,

But the snail was so slow . . .

. . . it took more than a day.

Betty was worried. "What's happened to Harry?
Where is the scarecrow I'm planning to marry?"

The farmer came by with a frown on his face,
And he made a new scarecrow to take Harry's place.

"Good day," said the scarecrow. "I'm Reginald Rake."
He took Betty's hand and he gave it a shake.

"Together," he told her, "we make a fine pair.
You're really quite pretty, apart from your hair."
Then he jumped in the tractor and told her, "Hop in.
I'm a really fast driver. Let's go for a spin."

But Betty said, "No — I must wait here for Harry.
He is the scarecrow I'm going to marry.
We're planning our wedding, the best wedding yet,
The wedding that no one will ever forget."

Reginald laughed. "You'll be waiting forever.
Forget about Harry! I bet he's not clever.

"I must be the cleverest scarecrow alive.

I can sing lots of songs. I can dance, I can drive!

I'm dashing! I'm daring! I'm cool as can be!

I can even blow smoke rings

   — just watch me and see!"

And he took out a big fat cigar from a packet
The farmer had foolishly left in his jacket.
"But smoking is *bad* for you!" Betty exclaimed.
"Really you ought to be feeling ashamed."

"Don't be a fusspot," said Reginald Rake.
"My smoke rings are staggering,
   make no mistake."
He struck up a light and he
   tried hard to smoke . . .
But straight away started to
   splutter and choke.

What happened next was completely unplanned:
The lighted cigar tumbled out of his hand.

It fell to the ground — and it started a fire.
Betty screamed, "Help!" as the flames flickered higher.

But Reginald Rake said, "I'd better be off,"
And he bounded away with a terrible cough.

Then suddenly,

who should appear on the farm

But Harry O'Hay,

with a pail on his arm.

"Betty!" cried Harry. "My own future wife!"

He poured on the water — and saved Betty's life.

Then they picked up the flowers, they hugged and they kissed,

A dress of
white feathers

a necklace
of shells

Lots of
pink flowers

two rings

and some
bells

And they said, "Now that's
everything crossed off the list."

So Betty O'Barley and Harry O'Hay

Wed one another the very next day,

And everyone (even the snail, who was late)

Said, "Don't they look happy?" and, "Don't they look great?"

"This," they agreed, as they sprinkled confetti
On Harry O'Hay and his beautiful Betty,
"Is the best wedding ever, the best wedding yet,
The wedding that no one will ever forget."

For Ally and Chris, and for Jerry and Teresa — J.D.

Scholastic Canada Ltd.
604 King Street West, Toronto, Ontario M5V 1E1, Canada

Scholastic Inc.
557 Broadway, New York, NY 10012, USA

Scholastic Australia Pty Limited
PO Box 579, Gosford, NSW 2250, Australia

Scholastic New Zealand Limited
Private Bag 94407, Botany, Manukau 2163, New Zealand

Scholastic Children's Books
Euston House, 24 Eversholt Street, London NW1 1DB, UK

www.scholastic.ca

Library and Archives Canada Cataloguing in Publication

Donaldson, Julia, author
The scarecrows' wedding / by Julia Donaldson ; illustrated
by Axel Scheffler.

Previously published: London: Alison Green Books, 2017.
ISBN 978-1-4431-4832-0 (softcover)

1. Readers (Primary). 2. Readers--Marriage. 3. Readers--
Agriculture. I. Scheffler, Axel, illustrator II. Title.

PE1119.D645 2018   428.6   C2017-907368-0

6 5 4 3 2 1   Printed in Malaysia 108   18 19 20 21 22